I'll Wait, Mr Panda

Steve Antony

What are
you making,
Mr Panda?

Wait and see. It's a surprise.

No, I will not wait.
Goodbye.

I'll wait,
Mr Panda.

Are you
making cookies,
Mr Panda?

Wait and see. It's a surprise.

Wait and see. It's a surprise.

Are you making cupcakes, Mr Panda?

No,
I'm done
waiting.

Is it ready yet, Mr Panda?

No, wait here.

I don't like waiting.

Goodbye.

I'll Wait,
Mr Panda!

I'm waiting, Mr Panda.

WOW!
That was worth the wait.

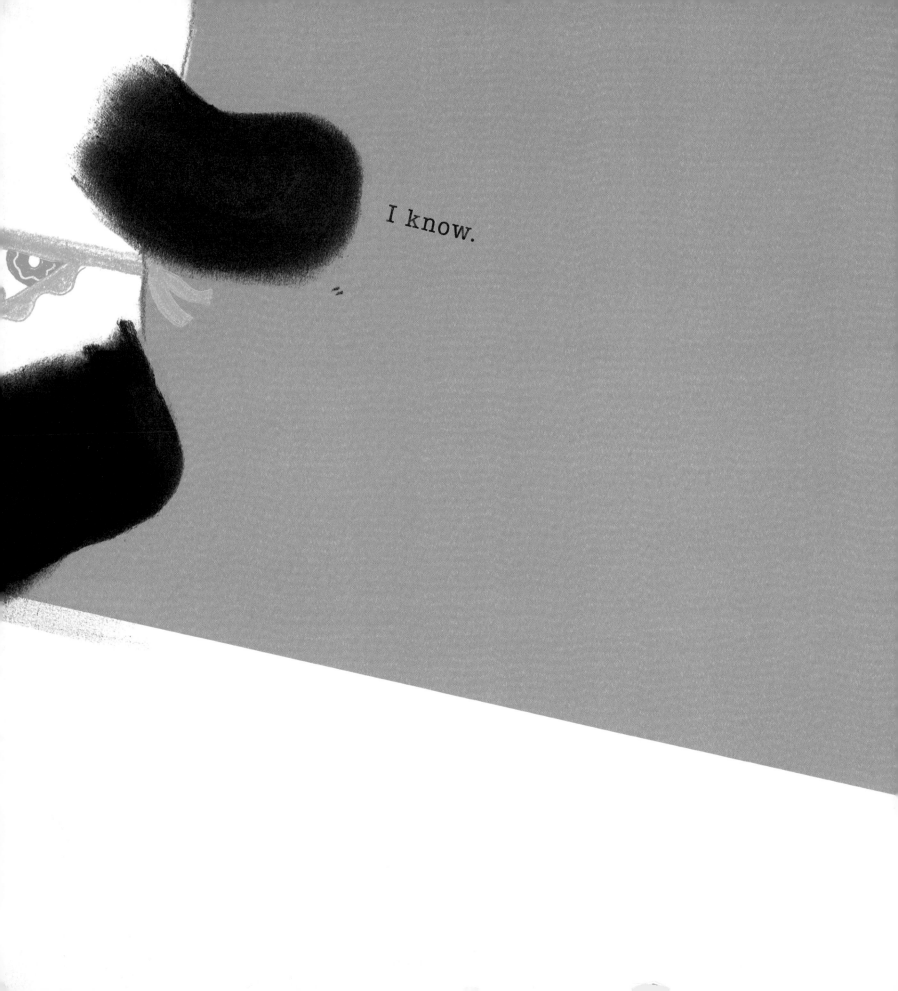

I know.

Thank you, Mr Panda.
I can't wait to eat it!

11.02.16,
Btw